Kids ask WHAT?

WHAT makes a cat's eyes glow in the dark?

WHAT is a blimp?

WHAT does a bulldozer do?

sequoia kids media

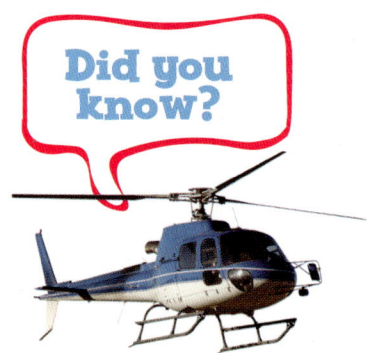

Illustrated by Linda Howard Bittner

Photography © Shutterstock 2021 JLStock (pg 4); Vadim Sadovski (p4); 3Dsculptor (pg 5); Denys Kurbatov (pg 6); Alexey Kljatov (pg 6); CGi Heart (pg 6); Daniel Prudek (pg 6); Peter Gudella (pg 6-7); Summer Photographer (pg 8); lunamarina (pg 9); EpicStockMedia (pg 10); Willyam Bradberry (pg 11); Andrew Sutton (pg 11); Coffeemill (pg 11); Anan Kaewkhammul (pg 12); Ultrashock (pg 13); bierchen (pg 14); Ralf Lehmann (pg 15); Valentin Valkov (pg 16); oksana2010 (pg 18); Ermolaev Alexander (pg 19); Photos SS (pg 20); KotukPhotography (pg 21); Nolte Lourens (pg 21); Kletr (pg 22); vvoe (pg 23); Nikki Zalewski (pg 24)

Published by Sequoia Kids Media,
an imprint of Sequoia Publishing & Media, LLC

Sequoia Publishing & Media, LLC.,
a division of Phoenix International Publications, Inc.

8501 West Higgins Road
Chicago, Illinois 60631

© 2022 Sequoia Publishing & Media, LLC

Sequoia Kids Media and associated logo are trademarks and/or registered trademarks of Sequoia Publishing & Media, LLC.

Active Minds is a registered trademark of Phoenix International Publications, Inc.
and is used with permission.

All rights reserved. This publication may not be reproduced in whole or
in part by any means without permission from the copyright owners.
Permission is never granted for commercial purposes.

Paperback edition published in 2022 by Crabtree Publishing Company
ISBN 978-1-6499-6698-8 Printed in China

Customer Service: orders@crabtreebooks.com

Crabtree Classroom
A division of Crabtree Publishing Company
347 Fifth Avenue, Suite 1402-145
New York, NY, 10016

Crabtree Classroom
A division of Crabtree Publishing Company
616 Welland Ave.
St. Catharines, ON, L2M 5V6

Table of Contents

What makes the moon shine?	4
What makes a rocket go?	5
What is snow?	6
What are mountains?	7
What makes soda pop fizzy?	8
What causes a burp?	9
What does a surfer do to surf?	10
What makes the ocean blue?	11
What happens when bears sleep all winter?	12
What makes a skunk stink?	13
What is a volcano?	14
What is lava?	15
What does a bulldozer do?	16
What does a crane do?	17
What makes a cat's eyes glow in the dark?	18
What do dogs dream about?	19
What is a helicopter?	20
What is a blimp?	21
What makes the sky turn different colors at sunset?	22
What is a seashell?	23
What makes the colors of a rainbow?	24

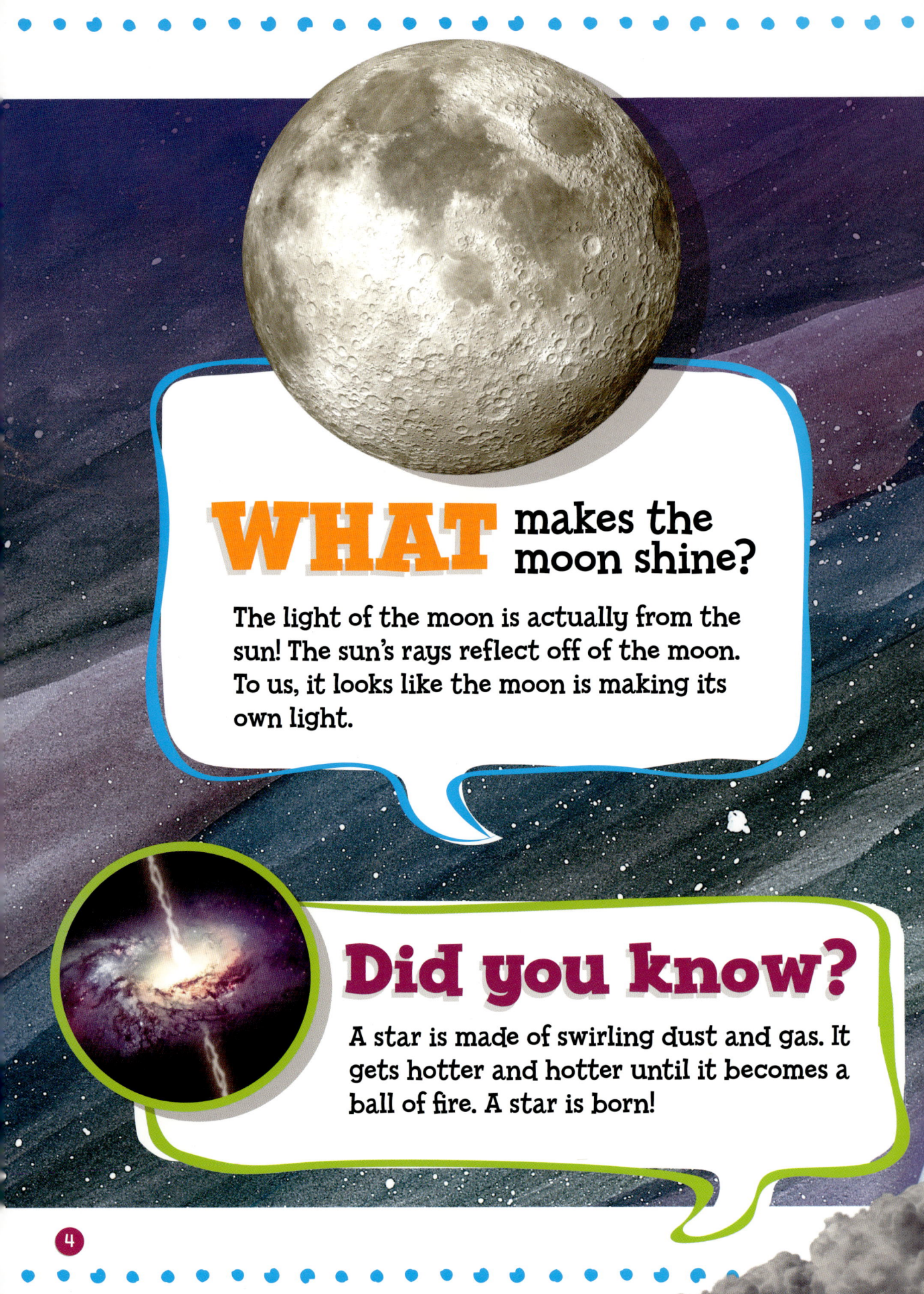

WHAT makes the moon shine?

The light of the moon is actually from the sun! The sun's rays reflect off of the moon. To us, it looks like the moon is making its own light.

Did you know?

A star is made of swirling dust and gas. It gets hotter and hotter until it becomes a ball of fire. A star is born!

WHAT makes a rocket go?

Rockets have engines, like cars and planes. Rocket engines make huge amounts of hot gas. The gas zooms down so fast that the rocket goes up.

WHAT is snow?

Snowflakes are made from tiny pieces of ice formed in clouds. Snow is mostly air, so a little bit of water makes a lot of snow.

Did you know?

The highest mountain in the world is Mount Everest. It is more than 29,000 feet high. That is almost as high as the highest airplanes fly!

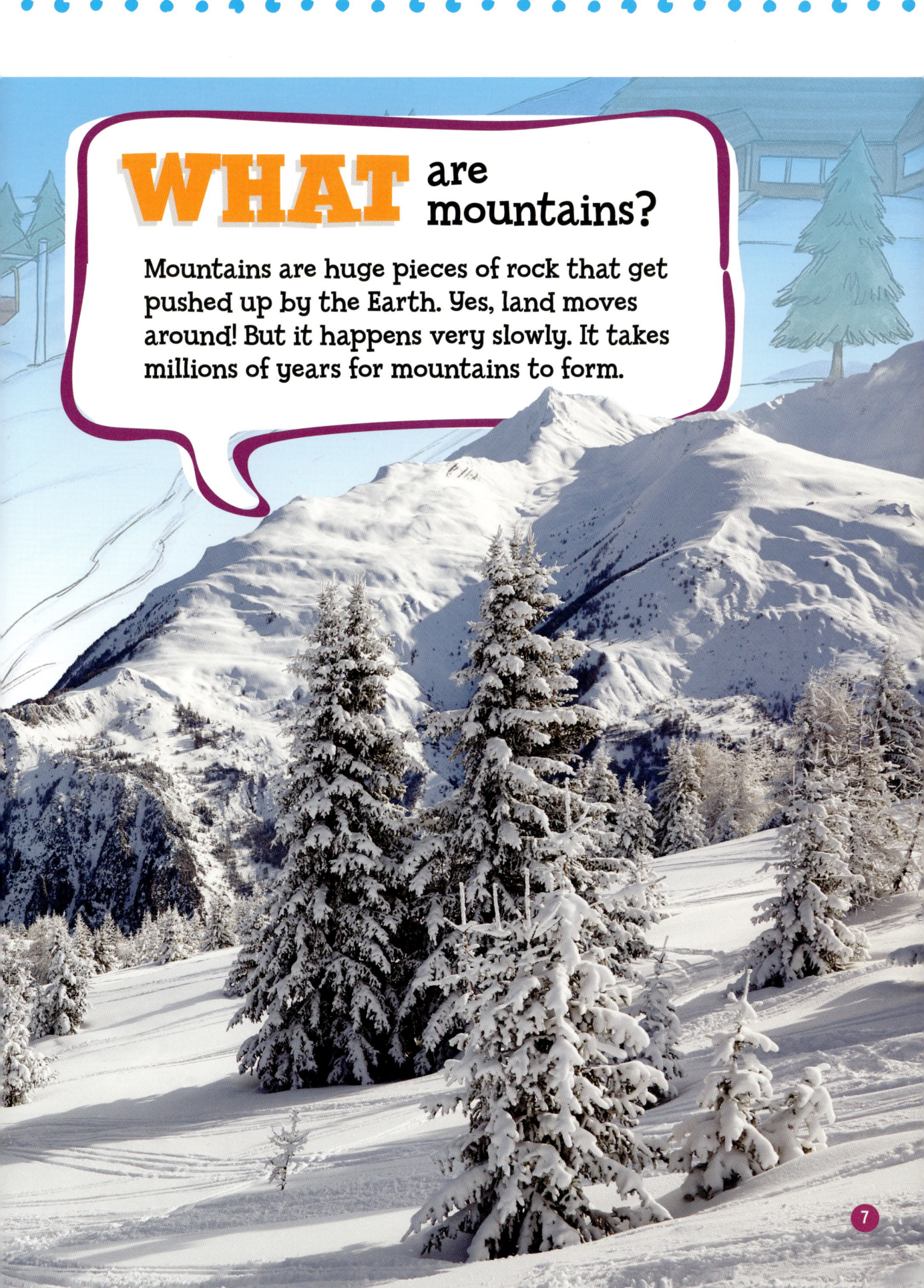

WHAT are mountains?

Mountains are huge pieces of rock that get pushed up by the Earth. Yes, land moves around! But it happens very slowly. It takes millions of years for mountains to form.

WHAT makes soda pop fizzy?

Soda pop has many tiny air bubbles in it. When you drink it, the bubbles pop in your mouth. You can see and hear the bubbles in a cup of soda, too.

Did you know?

You can get hiccups from drinking soda pop. You can also get hiccups when you are excited or are upset.

WHAT causes a burp?

When we eat or drink, we swallow air. Our bodies need to get rid of the air. A burp is air coming out of your mouth. Say, "Excuse me!" when you burp.

BURP!

WHAT does a surfer do to surf?

Surfers lie on their bellies on the surfboard. They use their arms to paddle to the part of a wave that curls over. The wave pushes them toward the shore, and they stand up!

WHAT makes the ocean blue?

Ocean water is mostly clear, but it reflects the sky. When the sky is blue, the water looks blue. The ocean can look many other colors!

Did you know?

The blue whale is the biggest animal in the world. It can weigh as much as 20 elephants!

WHAT happens when bears sleep all winter?

It can be hard for animals to find food in the winter. Bears hibernate to solve this problem. They sleep in a cave or a hole. Everything in their bodies slows down. When spring arrives, they wake up!

WHAT makes a skunk stink?

Skunks store a stinky spray under their tails. They spray when they feel scared. The smell can last for weeks!

WHAT is a volcano?

A volcano is a mountain with a hole in the top. The hole reaches deep into the Earth. When lava explodes out of the hole, it is called an eruption.

WHAT is lava?

The inside of the Earth is hot enough to melt rock! The melted rock is called lava. Lava burns everything it touches. When it cools down, it turns back into rock.

Did you know?

The biggest volcano in the world is Mauna Loa on the island of Hawaii. It covers half of the island!

WHAT does a bulldozer do?

Bulldozers push big, heavy piles of rocks and dirt from place to place. Their giant wheels help them go over the bumpy ground.

Did you know?

Some special bulldozers can work in the water. People drive them using remote control. That way no one has to get wet!

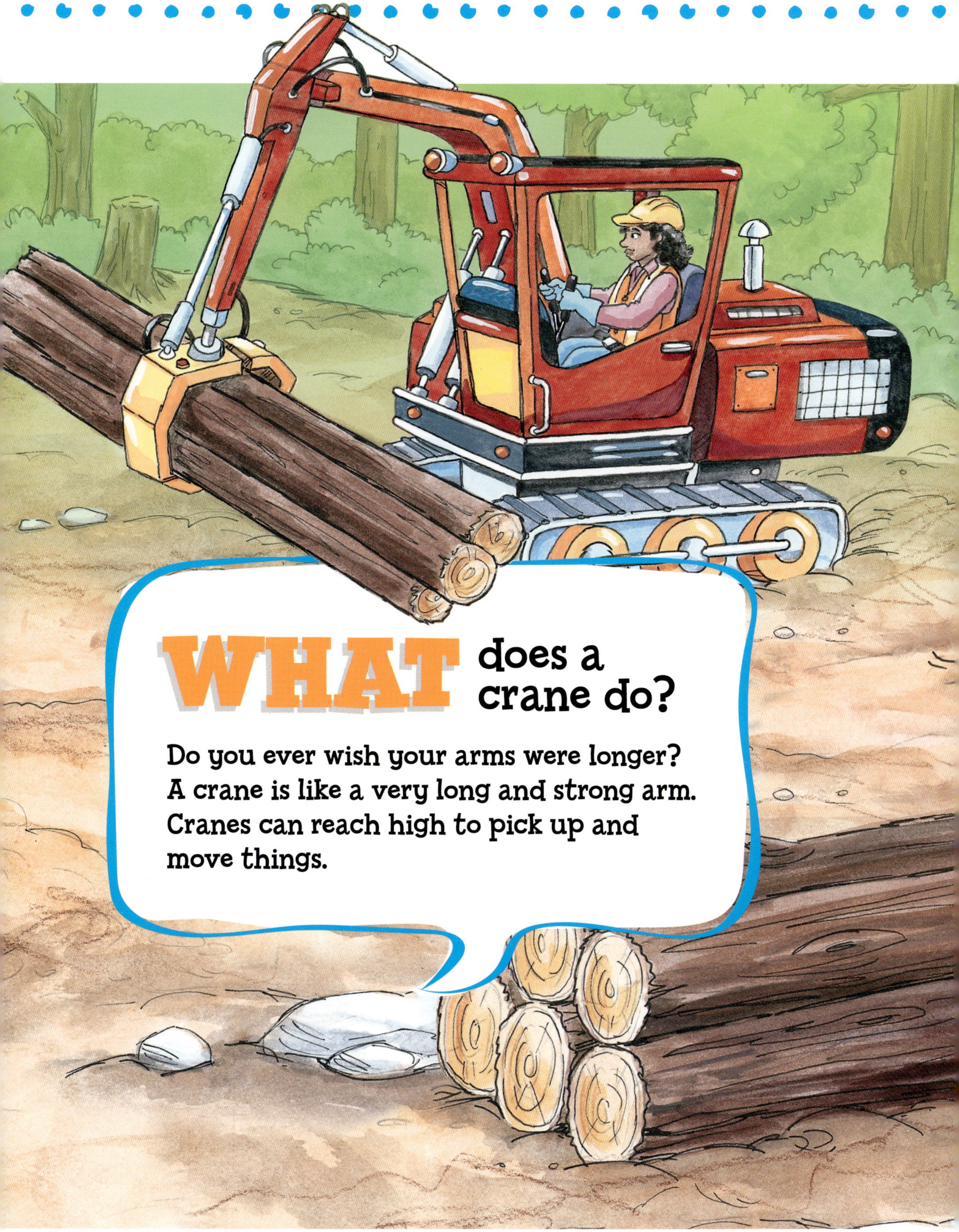

WHAT does a crane do?

Do you ever wish your arms were longer? A crane is like a very long and strong arm. Cranes can reach high to pick up and move things.

WHAT makes a cat's eyes glow in the dark?

Cats can see well in the dark. This is because their eyes reflect light like a mirror. We can see that light reflected in their eyes.

Did you know?

The biggest dog ever known was named Zorba. Zorba was as long as a horse and as heavy as seven kids!

WHAT do dogs dream about?

Scientists know that dogs dream. But they don't know what dogs dream about, since scientists don't speak Dog!

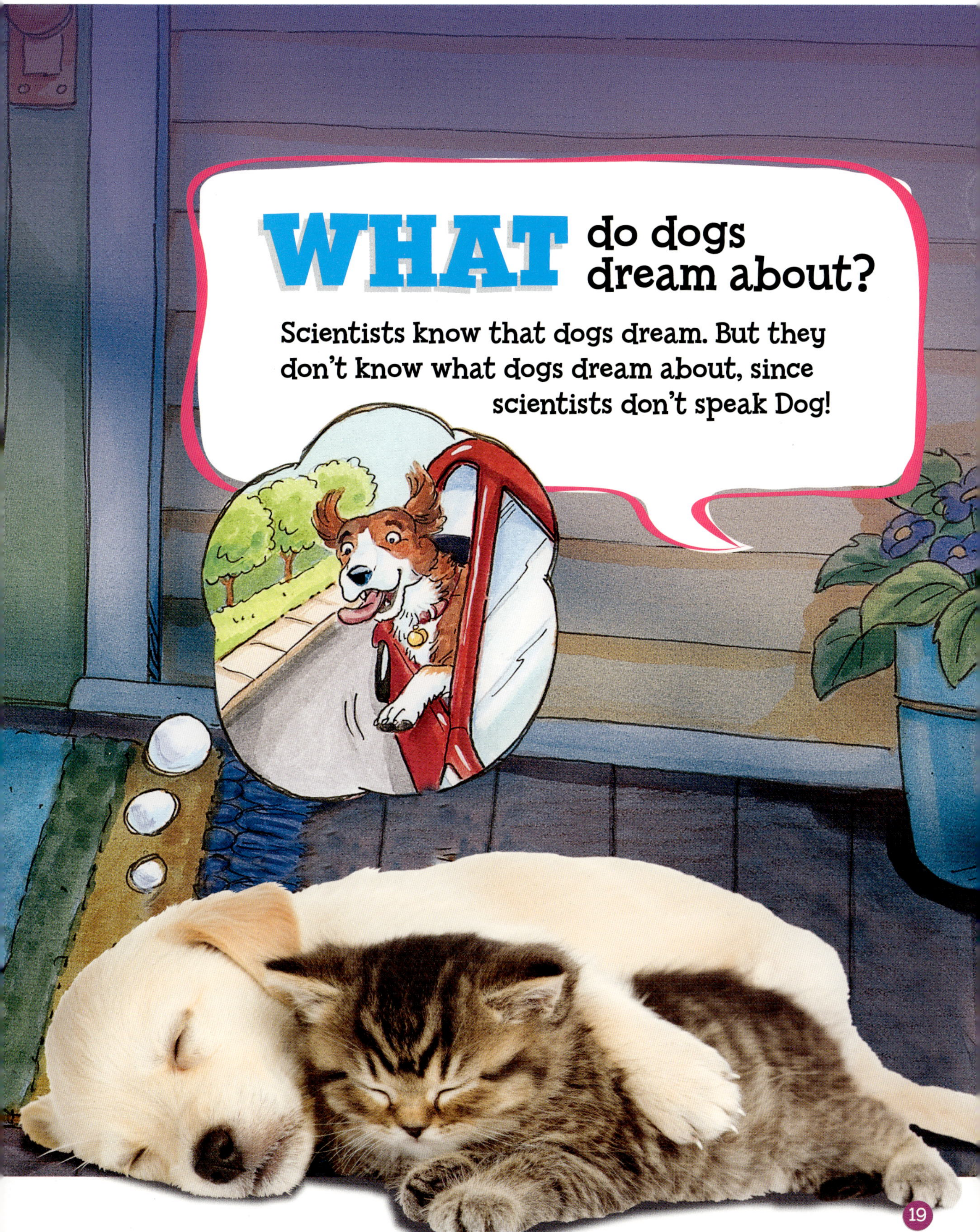

WHAT is a helicopter?

A helicopter is a machine. It can fly up, down, backward, forward, and sideways. It can also stay in one spot in the air!

WHAT is a blimp?

Blimps are giant balloons that people can ride in. They are filled with a type of gas that floats in the air—just like a party balloon.

Did you know?

Have you ever felt your ears "pop"? When you go up in an airplane, the air presses on your ears. Your ears "pop" so the air feels the same inside and outside.

WHAT makes the sky turn different colors at sunset?

Dust and water in the air can scatter light around. This causes the pretty reds, yellows, and purples we see at sunset.

Did you know?

It is fun to play in the sun, but don't look right at it. The sun is so bright that it can hurt your eyes.

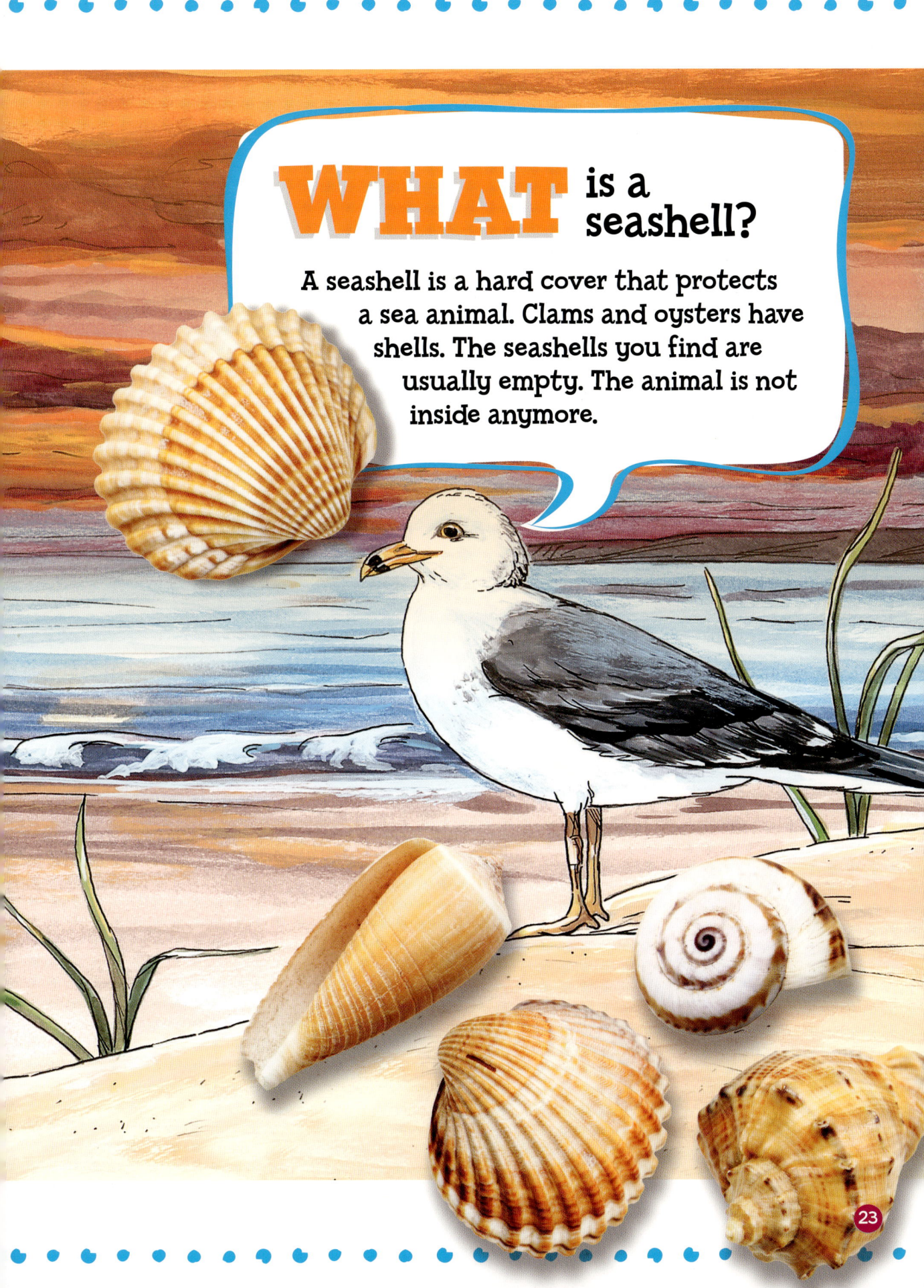

WHAT is a seashell?

A seashell is a hard cover that protects a sea animal. Clams and oysters have shells. The seashells you find are usually empty. The animal is not inside anymore.

WHAT makes the colors of a rainbow?

Light is made of many colors. We usually can't see light go through the air. But when the sun shines through raindrops in just the right way, we can!